Bootsie

you're 8

MIKE JAMES

Text copyright © Mike James 2011
Published by Vivid Publishing
P.O. Box 948, Fremantle
Western Australia 6959
www.vividpublishing.com.au

Check out: www.bootsiebooks.com for more information about the Bootsie Book series.

Chapters

1. Who's Bootsie?

2. "Bootsie, you're 8"

3. The Team

4. We Can Win This

5. Game Time

6. Quarter Final

7. Semi Final

8. Disaster

9. Nerves

10. The Western Rebels

1

Who's Bootsie?

This is the story of a boy who is known by everyone as Bootsie. Bootsie is 10 years old and plays for the South's Bulldogs under 11's Rugby Union team. He started playing for the Bulldogs when he was only 6. Bootsie has only missed one game since then and that was because he caught a cold from his little sister and was too sick to play. Bootsie loves under 11's because this year for the first time they are having proper scrums and lineouts. The Bulldogs have had a great season so far and are looking good for the Finals.

Of course Bootsie has a real name but people have been calling him Bootsie for so long I think they simply can't remember what it is. The teachers at school call him Bootsie, his Mum and Dad call him Bootsie, well at least until he gets in trouble and then his Mum will use his real name. Bootsie knows he is in big trouble when his

Mum calls him using his real name *and* middle name as well.

People haven't always called him Bootsie but each week from when he first started playing, he would turn up at rugby training with his rugby boots tied together by their shoelaces hanging around his neck. His very first coach, Mr O'Brian, would smile and say, "Ah Boots is here."

After a few weeks, during training, his new team mates would shout, "Pass the ball to me Boots." When Bootsie was running with the ball during a game one weekend, his team mate Stinkey (because he continually breaks wind) Taylor started shouting, "Bootsie, Bootsie, Bootsie pass it to me," and from that day on, all his teammates called him Bootsie. Even Mr O'Brian started saying, "Ah Bootsie is here," when he arrived at training. The name has stuck ever since that day.

At the dinner table that night after the game, his Dad said, "Pass the peas please Bootsie," as he looked down the table to his son. His Mum looked over at his Dad with a confused look on her face. "Who's Bootsie?" she asked him.

"The star player today, Bootsie," he replied, with a large smile on his face as he looked back at his son again.

"Oh yes, I forgot they were calling you Bootsie today," she answered. "Do you like that name?" she asked Bootsie.

"I guess so," he replied.

At school, soon after that day, Bootsie's teacher Mr Thomas, wanted to know what the terrible, strange odour he could smell in the class was. Stinkey Taylor quickly put his hand up and said, "It wasn't me sir. It was probably Bootsie."!

"Bootsie, and who is Bootsie?" Mr Thomas asked.

"Bootsie," replied Stinkey Taylor pointing towards Bootsie, trying to take the attention away from the real cause of the smell.

"Now now, Stinkey," replied Mr Thomas, "We don't need people to be pointed at, but next time can whoever made that terrible smell please go outside and do that.."

"Bootsie, can you open a window please?" asked Mr Thomas, "some fresh air in here would be nice.."

The class chuckled the first time they heard Mr Thomas call him Bootsie. Pretty soon, all his classmates started calling him Bootsie and not long after that, all his other teachers began calling him Bootsie as well. Then, the *whole* school was calling him Bootsie. Bootsie the name, was here to stay.

2

"Bootsie, you're 8"

It was a cold Saturday morning when Bootsie arrived at his home ground with his Mum, Dad and his annoying little sister, who had spent the entire trip to the ground, telling Bootsie how cold and wet it was going to be for him. Bootsie looked up at the sky and hoped that the clouds overhead didn't hold any more rain in them.

He looked around and could see some of his teammates across the field, so he ran off towards them.

"Bootsie," someone shouted. He looked back and saw his Dad standing next to the car holding his boots. "You might need these," he said. Bootsie ran back towards the car. "Oops," he said, "I'll need these today." He put his boots around his neck and ran off again towards his teammates who had seen him and were calling out his name. "Bootsie," he heard called out again. Bootsie turned around. "Good luck, hey," his Dad said, holding up his thumb. "Sure, thanks Dad," replied Bootsie.

As he ran towards his waiting team-mates, he could feel how wet and squishy the grass was, under his feet. *Yuk*, he thought to himself, as he arrived at the group of boys standing next to the coach. "Ah, Bootsie, you're finally here," said his under 11's coach, Mr Van Den. He was a huge man, who had played for his country in 7 test matches when he was younger. Coach Van Den started to hand out the jumpers.

"Stinkey, you're the hooker again. Get the number 2 jersey, hey," asked the coach. Stinkey just about dived into the bag to find his jumper. All you could see was a skinny pair of legs under a pile of jumpers. There were red, green and white striped jumpers flying all over the place and finally he shouted, "I found it.." Stinkey was so excited, he didn't notice the coach was now covered in most of the other jumpers he had just thrown backwards. "Thanks Stinky," Coach Van Den snarled.

"Ok Bootsie, you're 8," said the coach. "Nah, I'm 10," replied Bootsie.

"Listen to me, I am the coach and I'm telling you, you're 8," said his coach. "But Coach, I am 10, honest," replied Bootsie. "No young 'Super Boot'. Flyhalf Ben Smith over there, is 10 today," said the coach. "It's not my birthday," said Ben. "What?" asked the coach. "You said it was my birthday today and it's next week," Ben replied. "I didn't say anything about your birthday," said the coach. "Ok, I'm confused," he added. "Bootsie you're 8, and Ben you're 10," he said. "But *I'm* 10!" said Bootsie, "And *I'm* 9," added Ben with a confused look on his face. "9? You're not 9; our little halfback, Terry, 'the terrier' is 9," said the coach. Terry looked up from tying up the lace on his boot. "Who said I was 9?" he asked. "He did," replied Ben, pointing towards the coach. "But I'm 10," Terry said to the coach.

The coach's face started to get redder and his voice was getting louder, "Ok, for the last time, Bootsie you're 8, Terry you're 9 and Ben you're 10." "But, but, but," the boys tried to speak. "No buts about it. I am the coach and what I say goes, ok?" grumbled the coach. "And as for the rest of you, whatever I say your number is, will be your position for today and there will be no arguing like these three here.," he added. Bootsie, Ben and Terry looked at each other. "Oh! You mean *positions*, not *birthdays*," Bootsie said to the coach. "We thought you meant..." They started to laugh out loud. "Ok you three, I want you to do two laps for laughing and arguing with me. Off you go," he continued. Bootsie tried to speak, "But coach, we thought you meant..." His coach cut him off. "Two laps, I tell you, and *no* short cuts.."

Our halfback, little Terry whose nickname is the Terrier because when he tackles he hangs onto players like a little Jack Russell Terrier and gets dragged all over the field, started up again. "But Coach, we thought.." he was stopped mid sentence. "Do you want *three* laps?" snapped the coach. "Oh great," said Bootsie, as he grabbed Terry by the back of his jumper pulling him away. "C'mon lets start running before you get us any more laps." Ben, Bootsie and Terry started to run. "I think we had better play well today to make the coach happy," said Bootsie. "Yeah, he was getting pretty angry," Terry replied. The boys burst out laughing as they continued running. "Bootsie, you're 8," Terry said, as he continued to laugh and run at the same time.

Stinkey Taylor, who had pulled himself out of the empty bag of jumpers looked at the coach and said, "What are they running for?" The coach looked down at Stinkey, with one of the jumpers Stinky had thrown, still hanging over his shoulder. "As for you young Stinkey, you can join them," he said trying not to get even angrier. Just by the look on the coach's face, I think even Stinkey knew not to upset him any more and he took off after the other three boys who were a good distance ahead. "Hey you three, wait up," he shouted. Bootsie, Ben and Terry looked back. "Aagh! Stinkey's coming, run!" they cried.

3

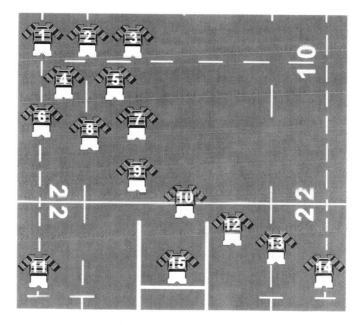

The Team

Just as the three boys were returning from running the two laps they could hear something approaching from behind them. Before Bootsie could look around, a flash went past him. "Helllooooo," said the flash as it continued running at warp speed. The boys looked at each other and said, "Red.." "Helllooooo," they heard again, as another flash went past them. "And Ted," they chuckled to each other.

Red and Ted were twin brothers, who were the fastest runners in the team and the entire school. At the school's sports carnival, it is always a race between these two to see who is the fastest runner in the school, even the older kids can't beat them. They are identical twins and are almost impossible to tell apart. They both have ginger hair, and freckles on their faces. Ted's real name is Edward, when the team found out that Ted is short for Edward, Red and Ted became their nicknames.

"We've nearly got a full team," said Terry, as the three boys walked the last few steps back to where the coach and the other players waited. The twins were catching their breath. "Hey, Red. Hey, Ted," the boys said on their arrival. "Hey," the twins said, as one. They always spoke at the same time, or one of them would finish the other's sentence. "My speedy wing-ers have arrived," the coach said. He threw a jumper to each of them. "Here, 11 and 14. Left and right wing, and I don't want any back-chatting about your birthdays or anything, you hear me?" snapped the coach. The twins were wondering what he was on about.. "He's still angry," Bootsie said to Terry and Ben.

"Now, where is the rest of the team?" the Coach asked. Stinkey Taylor came back after his run. He sounded like a train he was puffing so hard. "I'm... here.. Coach," he gasped. "I *know* you're here, I spoke to you earlier, you Muppet," relied the coach. "Where is my island connection?" he asked out loud. "We saw a car pull up over there when we were running. I think it might be them," said Bootsie, as he pointed to the other side of the field.

Ali and Tua were brothers who were born in Samoa. They moved here when they were only 6 months old and live near to where Bootsie lives. Ali is the older brother by 1 year. Tua is so big he plays a year above his own age group. Sunnie and Sione are Ali and Tua's cousins; they were also born in Samoa. They moved here only last year and came to play with the Bulldogs at the start of this year.

The coach's eyes lit up when he saw the boys coming across the field. "My island connection," he said, as they arrived. "Ali, loosehead or tighthead?" asked the coach. "I don't mind," Ali replied. "Ok, better make you tighthead," the coach said, as he threw Ali the number 3 jumper. "Guess that makes you loosehead, Tua," he continued, as he passed him the number 1 jumper. "Ali I think your brother is gaining on you, hey? Pretty soon he's going to be bigger than you," the Coach joked.

"Now my sizzling centre combination, Sunnie here, 12 for you, inside centre and 13 for you Sione, outside centre." The coach was beaming as he continued to command his troops.

The players who had arrived before Bootsie, were already given their jumpers. Coach Van Den's son, PK, who is the tallest player on the team is at second row. He was wearing number 4. A friend of PK's called James, was also in the second row, wearing number 5. James was also tall but not as tall as PK. Bootsie thinks PK will be taller than his Dad, who is huge. The rest of the team arrived one by one, Jamie 'mad dog' Jackson (he's a bit crazy) is the team's blindside flanker at number 6, and on the other side of the scrum is Mouse, who is the openside flanker wearing number 7. Mouse is so quiet, that when he talks, you can hardly hear him, but on the field, he is ferocious. The other team's fly half must have nightmares about him before the game. Mouse is always very polite and is one of the coach's favourite players, because he tries so hard.

'Sticks' McDonald plays 15 at fullback. He is the last man in defense and has got a great boot on him. He is a great player in defense, so when he shouts out, "mine," the team just lets him take the high ball. He rarely drops it. He may be skinny, but he plays really hard. He has thin white legs that look like sticks poking out from his shorts. When the boys asked him his name, he said, "You can call me Sticks, everyone else does." So they did.

As the clouds gathered overhead, a bus pulled up next to the field. "The other team is here," Stinkey shouted out. "Oh no, that's not them, they're huge. That must be the under 14 team," Stinkey added. "No it's not, said Bootsie. "That's the team were playing, I bet you." Bootsie suddenly felt a cold shiver run up his spine.

4

We Can Win This

The sky seemed to darken, as the other team made its way off their bus and towards the field. Bootsie's team had started warming up, with Bootsie and the forwards doing some lineout practice and the backs being led through some passing drills, by Ben the 'Super Boot' Smith.

"They are huge," said Stinkey, as the other team walked past them, whilst they continued their lineout practice. "C'mon Stinkey put the ball in," shouted PK. "They're not that big," PK continued. "Maybe not to you, you big ape," Stinkey replied. "What did you call me?" PK questioned. "Err nothing," replied Stinkey. "You called me a big ape, didn't you?" asked PK, as he began marching towards Stinkey. As he got closer to Stinkey, PK froze in one spot and started throwing his hands in the air. "Phwar, what's that smell?" PK shouted. "Oops sorry, baked beans for breakfast," replied

Stinkey with an embarrassed look on his face. PK backed up very quickly. "You're lucky, Stinkey," PK said to him, as he returned to his position in the line out. "Now put the ball in," he shouted.

The opposition coach and captain came over to Mr Van Den. The two coaches then shook hands. "Bootsie," shouted his coach, "Get over here," he continued. Bootsie ran over to where the two coaches were standing. "Yes Coach?" asked Bootsie. "This is the other team's captain and coach, now shake hands, hey." "Why?" asked Bootsie. "Because you're our captain today, that's why." "Oh," was all that Bootsie could get out. The referee tossed the coin and Bootsie called heads. "Tails it is," said the referee. We'll kick off," said the Warriors captain. "Ok, Warriors to kick off. Bulldogs, which end do you want?" the referee asked Bootsie. He froze. "Well, which end do you want?" the referee asked again. "W, w, we'll take the far end," he stammered. "Ok, Bulldogs get the far end in the first half. Good luck to both coaches and captains." said the referee, as he ran off to do his own warm up. The other coach wished Mr Van Den and Bootsie good luck and returned to his team, who had removed their tracksuits and were warming up in their white, blue and black playing jumpers.

Bootsie suddenly remembered this team, the Eastern Warriors. The Bulldogs had played them in round one earlier this year and the Bulldogs had been smashed. "What's wrong, Bootsie?" asked his coach. "Didn't you want to be captain?" he asked. "No it's not that. I'm just a bit..." "Nervous?" his coach asked. "How do you know?" Bootsie asked back. Coach Van Den looked at Bootsie and said "I wouldn't have picked you to be captain if I didn't think you could handle it Bootsie. If we make the finals then you will stay captain for the finals as well. Now go and talk to your troops, the game's about to start. Remember, stick to what we have done at training, and you will beat them." "Thanks Coach," replied Bootsie.

Bootsie ran over to his teammates. The team got into a huddle near the side line. "We can beat these guys if we just stick to what we have done at training, coach said to me." "Who made you captain?" said Stinkey. "Coach did," replied Bootsie. "I know we take turns each week, but for today, and if we make the finals, he wants me to do it. Ok?" Bootsie told his team. "That's fine by me. You are our best player after all," replied PK. "C'mon guys a good effort, and we'll be in the quarter finals next week, that's what matters," responded Bootsie. All the boys put there hands in the middle. "On three, one, two, three, Bulldogs!!"

The boys ran out onto the field and took their positions. Bootsie looked over at his mum and dad on the sideline. His mum was drinking a cup of tea from the thermos she had brought with her. Bootsie noticed the steam pouring out from the top of her cup into the cold air. His little sister was rubbing her arms against her long thick coat, teasing him about how cold he must be. Bootsie no longer cared about the cold or the wet grass. He wanted his team to be in the quarter finals next week, and nothing was going to stop him, except maybe the Warriors.

5

Game Time

"Warriors Captain, are you ready?" "Yes," was the reply. "Bulldogs Captain, are you ready?" the referee asked Bootsie, "Yes," he replied. Pheew! He blew his whistle and the game started. The Warriors fly half put up a high drop kick. "Mine," screamed Sticks, as he came running from full back, to take the ball. The Warriors players were charging after the ball. *Good luck, Sticks*, Bootsie thought to himself. Bumph, as the ball came down, it bounced straight off Stick's chest and onto the ground in front of him. "Aagh," shouted Sticks. Sticks jumped onto the ball on the ground in front of him. The referee blew his whistle. "Lost forward, green. Scrum to blue." "Sorry boys, I took my eye off it," he said as he got to his feet. "Don't worry Sticks, you tried your best." replied Bootsie.

"Ok boys, our first scrum," Bootsie shouted, as he tried to rev up his forwards. The referee set the scrum, Oomph!! A big hit, as the two front rows came together. "Heave!" Bootsie called, as he pushed from the back of the scrum. It didn't matter, the Warriors scrum pushed so hard they pushed the Bulldogs scrum until it collapsed. Bootsie looked up after being squashed by his own players, to see a Warriors player cross the line for an easy try under the posts. The first 5 points to the Warriors. The Bulldogs went back behind the posts in time to watch the Warriors fly half kick the ball for the conversion. The ball sailed through the posts. 2 more points. Warriors 7, Bulldogs 0.

The Warriors fly half sent up another high ball, this time it was coming straight towards Bootsie. "Mine," he screamed to his other players. Fortunately for Bootsie, the ball stuck to his chest. He looked up to see a huge Warriors player charging towards him. Bootsie side-stepped and the Warriors player missed him completely. He side- stepped around another player, and he was in the clear. Bootsie took off, with Sione alongside him, screaming for the pass. "Pass, pass, Bootsie," he yelled. Woomf!! Bootsie ran into a massive player from the Warriors and was tackled hard. "Lost forward, green," said the referee, "scrum down."As Bootsie got to his feet, it started to rain heavily. The referee set the scrum and again the Warriors smashed the Bulldogs' scrum. Bootsie looked up to see Red and Ted in pursuit of a Warriors player, but they couldn't catch him, and he scored, out near the wing. *12-nil,* Bootsie thought to himself. Luckily the Warriors kicker missed the kick at goal. Warriors 12, Bulldogs 0.

The rain got heavier and made the rest of the half, an ugly game. The ball was wet and got dropped all over the place. Bootsie was glad to get to half time and see if the coach could help the team. "Its ok boys, we've got another half to go," said Coach Van Den. "Now listen boys, it's wet out there, so hold onto the ball and drive it into them," the coach ordered. "Bootsie, I want you to come off the back of the scrum just like at training, ok," he added. "Yep," Bootsie replied. "It's too wet to pass it around too much, so hang onto it ok, now get out there."

"Remember boys, hang onto it, ok, just like Coach says," Bootsie said to his team mates, as they took to the field. Pheew! The referee blew his whistle and "Super Boot' kicked off, to start the second half. A Warriors player grabbed it and ran straight towards Bootsie. *Round the legs, round the legs*, he thought to himself. Smash!! A great tackle by Bootsie, the wet and slippery ball flew forward and PK jumped on it. "No advantage, we'll have a scrum," was the referees call. The scrum set, with Terry the Terrier to feed it. Just as he put the ball in, the momentum changed and woomf!! The Bulldogs scrum got smashed, again. The Warriors' coach must have told them a different strategy at half time, because they were throwing it around all over the field. They were doing some great, flashy passing, until once again, they were in at the corner for another try. *Goodbye quarter final,* Bootsie thought secretly to himself. The heavy rain made it difficult to kick, and the conversion at goal, missed by a mile. Warriors 17, Bulldogs 0.

'Super Boot' kicked off again, and Bootsie thought, *wow, look at Red run after that ball.* Red was off up the wing, with his eyes glaring at the ball as it travelled in the air. He leapt high in the air and boom! He came down with a thud, but at least he had the ball.

Ali and Tua came piling in to protect the ball. Little Terry dug around and came out with the ball, he dummied a pass to 'Super Boot' and he took off up the centre. The Warriors had no chance, they thought he was going to pass to the fly half 'Super Boot', and even *he* thought he was about to get it. Terry the Terrier, you champion, under the posts for our first try and 5 points. 'Super Boot' added the extras with the conversion. Warriors 17, Bulldogs 7.

The rain started to really pour down as the Warriors kicked off again. This time, Sticks took a lovely high ball and hung onto it, he took off and made it up to the half way line before he got smashed and lost the ball forward. "Scrum to the Warriors," was the referee's call. The scrum set. Smash!! Again the Bulldogs got hammered. Bootsie looked up to see the Warriors players running and passing. The Warriors player tried to pass to his open winger, but dropped the wet ball. It rolled forward right into Sunnie's feet. He picked it up and ran like the wind. Red and Ted are lucky Sunnie goes to another school, as he is pretty quick. The Warriors had no chance. Sunnie ran straight under the posts. Try! 'Super Boot' did the rest, and after a great conversion, the scoreboard read, Warriors 17, Bulldogs 14.

The game soon got messy again; in fact, it became a mud bath. Bootsie and the boys did some good work trying to hang onto the ball. The Warriors did the opposite, and kept passing wildly.

With only two minutes to go, one of their players threw a huge pass out wide, and James intercepted it. He was off, his big legs were powering up the field, and Bootsie was right behind him. He started to slow and was caught on the Warriors 22 metre line by the Warriors defender, who hit him so hard, he dropped the ball. The Warriors' player picked up the ball and was off. Bootsie, who was just behind James when he got tackled, wrapped up the Warriors' player's legs, and charged him into touch. "No advantage, we'll have a scrum for the knock on. Warriors feed, last play of the game," said the Referee.

Bootsie was charged-up after his tackle, "C'mon boys, one big scrum, that's all we need," Bootsie said to his forward pack. The scrum was set. "Heave," screamed Coach Van Den from the sideline. *Take it off the back of the scrum,* Bootsie thought to himself, *do what we do in training.* As the scrum set, Bootsie shoved himself into the back of the scrum. It was amazing, he could see the 22-metre line going behind him. "Push," he screamed, "we're winning, their scrums going backwards." It was. Bootsie could see the ball coming towards him. It went past PK's boots and was right under his feet. The ball was on the 5-metre line. Bootsie picked it up, and took off towards the try line. Two Warriors' players stood on the goal line, trying to stop Bootsie from scoring. He smashed through the middle of the two players, and was followed by the rest of his forwards. He was squashed, wet, dirty and tired, but he didn't care. He heard the referee's whistle. "Try!" the referee called, "to that player there." The referee pointed to Bootsie, still lying under a mass of bodies on the ground. With Bootsie's try, the score was 17 Warriors, 19 Bulldogs and the final siren had gone. The Bulldogs celebrated, "Great try Bootsie," someone said as he was patted on the back.

Ben 'Super Boot' Smith put the ball on his kicking tee; he took a few steps back. "*No pressure*" he thought to himself. "If I miss this we're still in the quarter final. He approached the ball. Boomph!! He kicked it perfectly, straight through the uprights anyway. *What a legend*, Bootsie thought to himself. Final score Warriors 17, Bulldogs 21. The referee blew his whistle "That's the game, Bulldogs win." Coach Van Den ran onto the field and hugged Bootsie, "Keep it in hand, run off the back of the scrum, see I told you," he said. "Quarter finals next week boys, quarter finals. Coach Van Den was very happy with the boys. Bootsie was so pleased to have won as captain *and* he scored the winning try. He didn't care who won the other match, he would find out next week. As he drove home with his excited parents, he just kept smiling. "Quarter finals." Even his sister was pleased for him.

6

Quarter Final

Bootsie lay in his bed and stared up at the ceiling in his bedroom. It was the Saturday morning after the win against the Warriors. "Please God, no rain," he said to himself out loud. "I got soaked last week, and I've still got bits of mud in my ears. Can we please have a dry game today?" he continued. He was almost too scared to get up and look out of his bedroom window. Bootsie slowly slid back his curtain and peered out; "Yes," he said excitedly. Not a cloud in the sky. "Thank you, God," you answered my prayers.

He ran downstairs to find his mum had cooked his favourite breakfast, bacon and eggs. "Ready for the game?" asked his dad, as he peered over the top of his newspaper. "Sure am, it's not even raining this week," Bootsie answered. Bootsie ate his breakfast and watched some cartoons on t.v. before he showered and changed into his rugby clothes, ready for the game.

"Are you ready already?" his sister asked. "Big game today," he replied. "Well, *I'm* going to a party, so I don't have to come," his sister snooted. *Cool*, Bootsie thought to himself. "Hey Mum, is that true, about the party?" "Yes, we'll drop her off first, then go to your game and be back in time to pick her up after the party" his mum answered. *Oh man, this day is starting out perfect*, Bootsie said to himself.

They dropped his sister off at her party and arrived at the ground with plenty of time to spare. Bootsie was so pleased to have the backseat to himself, without his annoying sister poking her tongue out at him, or something silly like she usually does. *Perfect, perfect*, he thought to himself.

He said goodbye to his parents and ran off to find his teammates. He had played at nearly all of the local clubs grounds before and he had definitely played here before. This was the home of the South East Cats, one of the South's Bulldogs closest rivals. There are two clubs near where Bootsie lives and they both have a team in the local competition. The Bulldogs are the older of the two clubs but the Cats formed shortly after. Almost 100 years ago. If you live anywhere near where Bootsie lives, then you're either a Bulldogs supporter or a Cats supporter. It's very simple, you're either a dog or a cat fan. There's a very fierce rivalry between the two clubs. Sunnie and Sione actually live closer to the South East Cats club, but play for the Bulldogs, because their Cousins Ali and Tua play for the Bulldogs. Next year, they are hoping to get a house closer to their cousins house and go to the same school as Bootsie and their cousins as well. Look out Red and Ted if they do, you boys will have some serious competition then.

Most of the boys were waiting for their game-day advice from Coach Van Den, as he hands out the jumpers, when Bootsie caught up with them. "Ah, 'Captain Courageous' is here," the coach joked. "Bootsie, you're 8, your jumper number that is," he laughed as he threw him his jumper. "I think we've found your position, hey," the coach added. "The captain, the general of the team, lead your troops from behind the scrum," he continued. "Sure thing, Coach" replied Bootsie. "We've just got to fatten you up a bit," his coach continued. Bootsie pulled up his jumper and stuck his stomach out as far as he could. "Plenty of bacon and eggs this morning," he laughed. Coach Van Den continued to pass out the jumpers to the other players and give tips and advice on their positions as he did. He was a great coach.

"Mad Dog and Mouse you're the flankers. As soon as that ball is out, you smash the fly half, ok. You don't wear number 6 and 7 for nothing. You're flankers. That's your job. Simple. And Mad Dog, no back-chatting the referee today, ok?" the coach said. "I don't want to lose this game on penalties. Terry my little number 9 halfback, when they've got the ball and it comes out of the scrum, I want you all over the other half back, ok. We don't call you the Terrier for nothing." "Sure Coach," Terry replied. "Where's my 'Super Boot' fly half? Aagh, there he is." He threw him his jumper. "You've got to have brains to play 10, you're the playmaker. Ben, lots of kicking today, hey. Nice and dry, good for a kicking game. Lots of high balls, put the defence under some pressure," he chuckled loudly. "And when that ball goes up, you two wingers, 11 on the left wing and 14 on the right wing, run like the clappers and put pressure on the defenders waiting to catch it. But make sure you're behind the kicker, when he kicks though, I don't want any offside calls, ok?" he said as he threw them the 11 and 14 jumpers. "Yes Coach" Red and Ted answered together.

"Where are my centres?" the coach looked around. "Here, 12 and 13 inside and outside. Inside number 12, Sione as soon as you receive the pass from the fly half, I want you straight down the centre, draw in a few defenders and bam!! Pass off to your Cousin Sunnic at outside centre wearing lucky 13, you here me" "Ah yep, sweet," Sione replied.

"What jumpers are left? 1,2,3,4 and 5. The tight five, the workhorse of the scrum! Stinkey, you make sure you put that ball in, straight at the line out, you hear. Now I used to be the hooker when I played, so make me proud. Go and practice throwing the ball at the

black dot on the crossbar over there."
The coach threw Stinkey his number
2 jumper, just like he wanted Stinkey
to throw the ball in at the lineout.

"Loosehead prop number 1 and my
tighthead prop number 3. Which one
of you boys is the biggest this week?"
he joked. "Now remember, good strong
scrums. Not like last week, when you
got pushed all over the field. And I
want you both to be first to the break-
down; you're the key to our rucks and
mauls. Ok. You're big strong boys, so
barge in there and clean out the opposition. Ok.," said the coach.

"Two more jumpers to go what have I
got here, 4 and 5. My second row, my
lock forwards. Good jumping at the
lineout today ok. Mix it up a bit, we
don't want them knowing which of you
is going to jump. Confuse them. And
push a bit harder than in the scrum
last week. We got pushed all over the

place, use your size. That's it, no more jumpers." The coach felt like Santa after he had given out all the presents. "What about me Coach?" asked Sticks McDonald. "Oh, wait a minute, what do I have here. One more, right at the bottom. Let me see. Number 15. How could I forget the fullback, our last line of defence. When all else has failed it's usually you in the backline, all alone trying to make a try saving tackle. A great effort under the high ball last week. I know you dropped an early one, but you put it behind you, and you took some real pressure ones. It wouldn't have been easy with that wet ball either, hey?" The coach asked Sticks. "Not at all," he replied. "It was like a wet bomb coming out of the sky," Sticks continued. "Ok, go and practice a few on your own before the game," asked the coach.

Whatever the coach said to his players as he gave out their jumpers that week sure must have worked, because the South's Bulldogs thrashed the South East Cats 45 to 3. They only got the penalty because Mad Dog couldn't help himself, and back-chatted to the referee. It had turned out to be a perfect day for Bootsie with another winning game as captain. Three tries for himself, as well as setting up Sione for his first try of the game. When they were driving home, his mum told him his sister was staying the night at her friend's house, so he could have one of his friends over to stay instead. *What a day*, thought Bootsie, *and next week, semi final!!!!*

7

Semi Final

The week since the quarter final seemed to drag on. Why is it, that when you're waiting for something good, it takes forever to get there, and when you know something bad is coming, like a visit to the dentist, it comes around really quick? Bootsie lay on his bed and prayed for good weather again. "Please God, can we have another perfect day like last week, I'll be good, I promise .Oh well, here goes," Bootsie said, as he walked over to his bedroom window. "Mmm not bad. Slightly grey, but I can see some blue bits," he said. He ran downstairs hoping it was bacon and eggs for breakfast, the same as last week. He ran into the kitchen, but there was no smell of cooking. "Where's Mum?" he asked his dad. "She's sick, up all night vomiting," his dad replied. "You'll have to have cereal today," he added. "This isn't starting out to be the perfect day I hoped for," Bootsie said to his dad. "Some days you're in front, some days you're not," his dad replied. "We'll have to take your sister and her friend to the game as well. Mum needs some rest," his dad added. Bootsie's good feeling about today was starting to slide away.

With his mum at home sick, Bootsie got to ride in the front seat with his dad. He liked the front seat, and his dad let him choose the music on the radio. He also liked the fact that he didn't have to share the back seat with his sister and her equally annoy ing friend.

They arrived at the South's Bulldogs home ground, and Bootsie looked around for his teammates. After a while he noticed Sticks with his dad and a few others, near the clubhouse. "No Coach today," said Sticks. "What!" replied Bootsie "He's sick, up all night, vomiting," Sticks said. "Me and my dad went there this morning to pick up PK and the jumpers." "Oh no, this is terrible," said Bootsie, "who's going to be coach?" "Maybe your dad could do it?" said Sticks' father. "What did he say?" Bootsie asked Sticks. "He said maybe your dad could do it," replied Sticks. "What, my dad?" Bootsie asked. "Why not? I played a bit in my day," replied Bootsie's dad. "Yeah, but not test rugby, like Coach Van Den," replied Bootsie. "Beggars can't be choosers, Bootsie," his dad replied. "What does that mean?" asked Bootsie. "It means you can't be too choosy, when you've got nothing to choose from," said Stick's dad. "What did he say?" Bootsie asked Sticks. "What, are you deaf, Bootsie?" replied Sticks. "It means we have to make do with what we've got," Sticks added. For some reason Bootsie always had trouble understanding Sticks' dad's accent, as he was born in another country.. "What about the advice our coach gives to each player every week?" Bootsie asked his Dad. "We'll just have to do without it this week, I'm sure if your coach could be here he would, he must be very sick," replied Bootsie's dad. "Yeah he's pretty sick," added PK, who was listening to the conversation. "Red's sick too, his Mum rang the house this morning and said he wasn't coming," PK added. "Oh man, this is great, no coach and now one of our wingers isn't coming," cried Bootsie. "What about my prayers, God?" Bootsie asked as he looked up to the darkening sky. "Now now Bootsie, the Lord works in many mysterious ways, you can't blame him for this," said Bootsie's dad.

Bootsie had never played in a grand final and he was starting to wonder if he would be playing in one next week, especially when Stinkey Taylor rolled up looking very ill. "Not you too?" Bootsie said, as he got closer. "Oh man, my stomach hurts bad," Stinkey said to Bootsie. "I just can't stop, pl-plplplfffff" "Oh Stinkey, that stinks," said Bootsie, as he waved his arms around like he was near a bees' nest. "I know," said Stinkey. "They're worse than normal," Stinkey added. "Well we've got to make the best of it. I'm glad you came, but if you're too sick, don't play," Bootsie said. "I'll be Ok," replied Stinkey. "Well you'd better tie up your laces Stinkey, they're both undone," said Bootsie. "Oh ok," replied Stinkey, as he looked down and noticed his untied laces.

The referee came over to Bootsie and his dad, "Are you the coach?" he asked Bootsie's dad. "I guess so," he replied. "Ok, this is the Eastern Warriors coach and captain," said the referee. "Oh ok," replied Bootsie, feeling a bit strange that he had never seen this player before. The Bulldogs won the coin toss and Bootsie told the referee that his team would kick off. When the other coach and captain left, Bootsie turned to his dad and said, "I've never seen that kid play for the Warriors before." His dad responded "Maybe he's new." "But we played them two weeks ago, and he didn't play in that game," Bootsie added. "I don't know," his dad said. "I know they were second on the ladder and that's why they're still in the finals. I don't think they were too happy about losing to us the last time we played them," his Dad added. "C'mon tiger," his dad said, as he put his arm around Bootsie's shoulder. "You guys beat them two weeks ago, they're not unbeatable." "My dad's right," said Bootsie, "We've beaten them before, we can do it again." The Bulldogs ran onto the field full of new hope.

It's lucky for Bootsie that he won the coin toss because that's all the Bulldogs won that day. From the first kick, the sky opened and it poured down, turning the South Bulldogs' ground, into a mud bath. Bootsie and the boys tried so hard, but with Coach Van Den and Red missing, it made the day even harder. At half time, the score was, Warriors 21, Bulldogs 0. "They're huge, some of these boys," said Stinkey, at the half time break. "I agree," replied PK. "If you think they're big, they must be," Bootsie said to PK. "Some of these boys didn't play for them two weeks ago," PK said to Bootsie. "I'm getting smashed," added Stinkey. "Well, you could at least tie your laces Stinkey, I told you already, they were loose," replied Bootsie. "Lets just do our best, if we don't make the final, we've done well to get this far," Bootsie said to his teammates.

The start of the second half seemed promising for the Bulldogs, Bootsie did a great solo effort to score under the posts, and 'Super Boot' kicked the conversion. Warriors 21, Bulldogs 7. Sione and Sunnie did some great passing to each other up the centre, and with a quick pass, put Mouse over the line, just after Bootsie had scored. 'Super Boot' did the rest, and the score looked a little better. Warriors 21, Bulldogs 14.

At one point, the scores were nearly level when Stinkey Taylor intercepted a Warriors pass, and was off up the wing with no Warriors players even close to catching him. If only he'd tied his boot laces, like Bootsie had told him, he wouldn't have tripped over himself and lost the ball forwards. As far as the Bulldogs score was concerned, that was it for today, 14. The Warriors had a different story. They ran in numerous trys and the score blew out to Warriors 55, Bulldogs 14. In some ways, Bootsie was pleased to hear the siren. They had been smashed in the wet by a much bigger team, and the Bulldogs had played pretty well considering they were one player short, and were missing Coach Van Den.

Bootsie walked over to where his dad was standing. "Good game mate," said his dad, as he patted Bootsie on his shoulder. "Some of them were just too big," replied Bootsie. As Bootsie was talking to his dad and the other boys, PK's older brother, AJ, came to get PK. "How did it go?" AJ asked Bootsie and PK. "We got smashed," replied Bootsie and PK at the same time. "Not by the boys over there, I hope," AJ said, as he pointed to the Warriors team, who were celebrating their win. "Yep that's the ones," replied Bootsie. "Why?" Bootsie asked AJ. "My under 14's team beat the under 14's Warriors team two weeks ago, and they didn't make the finals. Some of the boys over there were in that team. Some of the boys you played against today are 13." "Are you sure?" Bootsie's dad asked AJ. "Positive," AJ replied. "Well, we'll soon see about this," screamed Sticks' dad, who seemed quite mad about it. "What did he say?" Bootsie asked Sticks. "He said we'll see about this," replied Sticks, "C'mon Bootsie, he's not that hard to understand," Sticks added.

Bootsie's dad, AJ, Bootsie and Sticks' dad went over to the referee, to tell him about what was going on. The referee said he thought something was wrong, because of the size of some of the boys playing for the Warriors. He called the Warriors coach over. "I want to see your players' sheet," the referee said to him. "My err what?" he replied. "You know, the list of players playing for your team today; some of them seem a lot older than they should be." "Ok it's my fault," the Warriors coach said. "Some of my players are sick, some stomach bug or something. I took some players from the under 14's competition who's season has finished, and put them into the team. I just wanted to win, no harm done, nobody got injured, did they?" The Warriors coach asked. "Well, they could have," replied Bootsie's dad to the other coach. "What happens now?" Bootsie asked the referee. "It means the Warriors are disqualified and Bulldogs move into the 'Grand Final' next week." "Say that again," Bootsie asked the referee. The referee put his hand on Bootsie's head and said, "Congratulations. The Bulldogs are in the 'Final' next week." Bootsie jumped in the air "Yahoo," he shouted. He ran over to his teammates to tell them the great news. They were so excited to be in the 'Grand Final'. "Who are we playing?" asked 'Super Boot'. "I don't know, I forgot to ask," replied Bootsie. "Hey ref," Bootsie shouted, "Who are we playing next week?" "The Western Rebels, I think," was the referee's reply. Bootsie looked at his teammates who all looked very pale; "The Western Rebels," Terry gulped. "Remember what happened last time we played them?" said PK. "Oh yes I remember," said Bootsie, "I remember."

Disaster

"Aagh," Bootsie's mum screamed out from the laundry room. "Are you ok?" his dad asked. "Yes, but you might want to see this," she replied. Bootsie's dad went into the laundry, "Oh dear," he gasped. "That's a nice shade of pink," his dad said to his mum. "I don't know what happened," she replied, as she continued to pull bright pink rugby jumpers out of the washing machine. "I've washed the boys' jumpers heaps of times and this has never happened before." "Oh hang on," she said, this might be the problem. She reached deep into the washing machine and pulled out Bootsie's sister's favourite dolly. "It looks like the dye from her hair has all come out in the wash, her hair's not red any more, it's blond," his mum said to his dad. "How are we going to tell Bootsie about this?" his dad wondered. "Tell me what?" came the reply from Bootsie, who had come downstairs to get a drink. "Aagh, the jumpers they're p, p, pink." Bootsie looked very pale. "Your sister's dolly ended up in the wash somehow, and the dye from her hair has leaked out." Bootsie ran into the lounge room where his sister was playing with her other dolls. "Did you put that dolly with the red hair in the washing machine?" he asked angrily. "Yes, she's having a bath," his sister replied. "Well it's turned all the team jumpers pink," Bootsie snapped. "Ok Bootsie, it's an accident. She didn't do it on purpose," his mum said, as she entered the lounge. "I know, but how can we play a grand final wearing pink jumpers?" he asked his mum. "I don't quite know yet," his mum replied.

Bootsie sat at the table and tried to eat his bacon and eggs, but he felt sick in his stomach. "Pink jumpers," he said to his dad. "Yes Bootsie, I know," his dad replied, "Maybe there's some old ones at the club we could use," his dad added. "No there's not. These are the only ones we've got," was Bootsie's response. As they drove to the ground, Bootsie sat and watched his sister brush the now blond hair of her favourite dolly, over and over again. "Pink jumpers!" he said to her. "Well I think they're a nice colour now," his sister snooted. "You would. You're a girl," Bootsie quickly replied. "You're supposed to like pink," he added harshly. "Easy son, easy," his dad said from the front seat, we're here now anyway."

The Western Rebels Rugby Club or Rebels as they are known, have a massive flag flying from the top of their club house. Their flag is black with a large white skull and crossbones image right in the middle of it. Even hearing the name of the club, made Bootsie's skin tingle. The club colours are black and white just like the flag. Bootsie hated this club, and hated this ground. Earlier in the season, he had been hit so hard in a high tackle by their hooker, he had to go off injured and still can't remember much of the game. The area near their home ground is a pretty rough neighbourhood. It's not too far away from where Bootsie lives, but is far enough away that he doesn't have to go to any of the schools near it, which suits Bootsie fine. Some of the boys who play for this team, are mean and huge.

"Mum, I feel sick," Bootsie said to his mum as his dad dropped the bag of jumpers onto the ground near Bootsie's feet. "You'll be ok," she said, "It's only a colour." The rest of Bootsie's teammates soon gathered around the bag of jumpers, which Bootsie had tightly sealed. Coach Van Den arrived, and stood next to the bag, "Err Coach, I need to tell you something," Bootsie said, looking up at him. "Ok Bootsie, in a minute. Let's do the jumpers first, hey," he replied. "The Rebels said we can use the change rooms today, seeing as it's a grand final so come on everyone into the visitors change rooms. I'll hand out your jumpers in there," continued the coach. The boys all assembled into the change rooms, it had a strong smell of menthol from the rubbing lotions the older players rubbed on any sore spots they might have. His coach spoke, "Now I'm sorry I wasn't here last week, but I was terribly sick. Must be the wife's cooking, hey," he joked to Bootsie's dad, who was standing near by. "I heard you boys played well without me, and I'm really pleased we are here today. Ok jumpers, what number jumper do we have first?" Coach Van Den unzipped the bag. "Oh dear me," he gasped. "What has happened here?" he said, as he started scratching his head. "My dolly's hair made them pink," Bootsie's sister told the coach. "It certainly has," the coach said to Bootsie's little sister, who had made her way into the change room. A huge gasp was made when all the boys realized what the coach had pulled out of the bag. "Are they our jumpers?" Terry the Terrier asked. "I'm not wearing one of them," Mad Dog said. "Well we have no other tops, so you will be wearing it," the coach replied gruffly. "And I don't want any thing else said about them today. You hear me?" the coach added. The boys realized by the tone in his voice he didn't want to hear any more complaining about it. He passed out the jumpers to the players one by one. "We look like a bunch of girls," Stinkey said to Mouse. "Who said that?" the coach asked. "I did," said Stinkey. "The next boy I hear complain, will be doing laps. You hear me?" he added.

The referee came into the change rooms, "Game's about to err, whoa, sorry, I meant the game's about to start. Good luck out there, I think you might need it." The boys heard a massive cheer from the local crowd as the Rebels ran onto the field wearing their all black uniform with just some small white stripes on the shorts and socks. "Ok boys, off you go," said Coach Van Den. None of them moved. "C'mon, you can't stay in here all day," he continued. The boys ran out of the change room onto the field. The crowd was still cheering for the Rebels players, when the Bulldogs ran out, but suddenly it all went very quiet. There was a long pause. The boys froze as they felt the crowd's eyes staring at them. "Ha Ha, nice tops boys," one person laughed. That was it. Then the whole crowd started laughing and pointing. The Rebels players were rolling around on the ground, holding their stomachs, they were laughing so hard. "No," said Bootsie, "No, No, No," he continued. Bootsie felt a hand on his shoulder and he started to shake. "Bootsie," he heard his mum's voice. "No, No, No." "Bootsie, Bootsie, Bootsie."

9

Nerves

"Bootsie, Bootsie." He felt his body shake. "Wake up dear." "Err what?" said Bootsie. "I think you were dreaming," his mum replied. "You were shouting out about pink jumpers, and kept saying no, no, no." Bootsie looked up from his sleepy eyes, "Oh man Mum, I'm so glad it's you. I was dreaming about...." "About what?" his mum asked. "Just a sec," said Bootsie, as he jumped out of bed and ran down the stairs. "Are you Ok, Bootsie?" his Mum asked, as she raced down the stairs behind him, wondering why he was in such a rush. Bootsie ripped open the lid of the washing machine, "Where are they?" he asked. "What?" his Mum replied. "Our rugby tops." "Oh, they're in the dryer, nearly ready." Bootsie reached up and opened the dryer door; he reached inside and yanked one of the jumpers out, pulling most of the other ones with it. "Oh thank you," he said, as he rubbed his face into the fabric of one of the jumpers. "They're red and green just like they should be." "Of course they're red and green," his mum said. "What colour did you think they were, pink?" she added. Bootsie sat on the floor and started laughing; once he started he couldn't stop. "Are you Ok?" his Mum asked, "Yes, I'm fine now," still laughing. "It's just, never mind," he said. "Oh, ok then, if you say so," his Mum replied. Bootsie's sister walked into the laundry to see what he was laughing at, she was holding onto her favourite dolly, the one with red hair. When Bootsie saw it, he laughed even harder. "Well I'm glad you're so happy today, Bootsie," his Mum said. "Don't forget you're playing your grand final today." Bootsie stopped laughing immediately, and sat bolt upright. *The Western Rebels,* he said to himself,

"Oh man I feel sick all of a sudden." Bootsie shrieked, as he ran off towards the toilet.

"Oh Mum, I don't feel good," Bootsie said, as he sat at the breakfast table, eating his bacon and eggs. "It's just nerves, that's all, it will pass," his mum replied. "I hope so," he said, as he took off towards the toilet again. "Pre-game nerves I think," Bootsie's dad said, as he lowered his newspaper. "I think you're right," replied his mum. "C'mon Bootsie, we'll be late," shouted his dad. Bootsie could hear the car engine running outside, as he sat on the toilet again. His dad came inside and tapped on the toilet door. "It's ok son, it's only nerves. It's natural before a big game. "I know, just give me a sec, and I'll be out," came the response from behind the toilet door. Bootsie made his way out to the car. "It's about time," his sister said. "Dad said he'd thought you'd fallen in," she added. "C'mon Bootsie, you'll be right once you get there," his dad said.

The Western Rebels had won the grand final for the last three years running and they had beaten the Bulldogs 30 nil earlier this season. Bootsie was worried today might be a similar result. They had a real mean hooker on their team, who Stinkey was terrified of. Earlier in the year ,he tackled Stinkey so hard, Stinkey was taken off for the rest of the game. Just like Bootsie, he dreaded facing that hooker again.

"We'll be cheering for you," said Bootsie's mum and dad, as he ran off to find his teammates. "Thanks," he replied. As he ran, Bootsie was still worrying about their hooker, as well as the rest of the Western Rebels. "Lovely, my captain is here at last," said Bootsie's coach, as he arrived next to the other boys. "Good, you're the last one. We have a full team," the Coach continued. "Ok, before I start does anyone need to go to the toilet?" "I do," said Bootsie. "Well off you go then," replied Coach Van Den. "Me too," said Terry. "And me," said 'Super Boot'. Pretty soon all the boys had run off in the direction of the toilets until Coach Van Den was standing all alone next to the bag of jumpers at his feet. When the boys returned the Coach sat them down in front of him and started his pre-game talk. "So you're all a bit nervous? Your stomachs have butterflies in them? That's perfectly normal, Ok. They will make you play better, believe me. Nerves make you play better. I would be more worried if you weren't nervous. When I played in the test matches I spent as much time on the toilet before a game as I did playing in the match. Once the game starts, you watch those nerves disappear," he said. "These Rebels are only boys like you. They're no different. They will be as nervous as you boys are feeling right now. The hero and the coward are both the same, they both are nervous before whatever it is they have to do, but it's what the hero does that makes him a hero and what the coward does that makes him a coward. In time you will come to understand this. I hope. We can win this game today, I believe in you boys, and I mean it. You've heard me tell you all year that all you have to do is to believe in yourselves and anything is possible. Now get out there and show me what you can do." Coach Van Den's speech had really fired up the Bulldogs; deep down Bootsie knew if everyone put in their best effort the Bulldogs could beat the Rebels. Now they had to prove it. The referee blew his whistle and the grand final game was on.

10

South's Bulldogs

Rugby Union FC

V's

Western Rebels

Rugby Union Club

In this year's under-11's Grand Final.

The Western Rebels

The referee blew his whistle and the under-11's grand final was under way. 'Super Boot' started the game with a huge drop kick for the South's Bulldogs. "After it! After it! Chase it up!" Coach Van Den shouted to the players. Ted took off down the right wing. Wow, he was fast. He caught up with the ball just as the Rebels' player caught it on his chest. He tried to run, but 'Pow', Ted tackled him and the Rebels player fell to the ground. "Let go of it!" the referee said to the Rebels' player who was waiting for his support to arrive. 'Pheew', the referee blew his whistle. "Not releasing the ball.– Green player was on his feet: he's allowed to play the ball, he's the tackler, he stayed on his feet and there was no ruck formed, penalty to green." he said. "Great work, Ted," shouted Coach Van Den from the sideline, and he raised his thumb in the air. "Captain what do you want?"

the referee asked Bootsie. "Um, we'll take the kick at goal thanks sir," he replied. The referee pointed to the posts with both hands. 'Super Boot' came to the spot with his kicking tee, he set the ball up, took a few steps back and 'Woomph', off it sailed straight between the uprights. Rebels 0, Bulldogs 3.

The first half was flying by; Bootsie's butterflies had flown away as soon as that first whistle was blown, Now he was more worried about winning this game and beating the Rebels. Sticks took care of the high drop kick after the restart. "Mine," he shouted as he took it on his chest. He stayed inside his 22 and booted it way up field and over the touch line near Bulldogs 10-metre line. The lineout was set. PK and James were excellent jumpers and did well to steal the ball back into the Bulldogs' possession. Terry the

Terrier grabbed the ball from out of the maul and passed it out to the fly half. 'Super Boot' ran a few metres and dummy-passed which fooled the first Rebels' defender. He slipped a pass to Sunnie who was playing inside centre. Sunnie did well and got the Bulldogs up to the Rebels 22-metre line only to be brought down in a hard tackle. He did well to hang onto the ball just long enough for the two props Tua and Ali to arrive and smash themselves into the ruck. Little Terry the Terrier dug around, dragged the ball out and passed it to Bootsie. Bootsie ran towards the try line. he tucked the ball under his arm and pushed off a defender with his other hand. He ran a few more metres and was dragged to the ground right next to the goal line he reached over and put the ball on the try line. 'Pheew'. "Try!" the referee shouted, "Try to number 8!" Bootsie was so happy, he ran back to the halfway line and noticed the player he had pushed over was the Rebels' hooker that had flattened him in the last game. He didn't look so mean now, Bootsie thought to himself as he rejoined his teammates. Another perfect kick from 'Super Boot' and the score was Rebels 0, Bulldogs 10. "Great start boys," Bootsie shouted to his teammates, "let's keep this up!."

Bootsie could see the hooker was back on his feet and glaring at him. He didn't care. "I pushed you over once and I'll do it again," Bootsie said to himself. The game restarted and the ball sailed towards Stinkey, "Yours, Stinkey," Bootsie shouted, as the ball came closer. But Stinkey froze and let the ball bounce, "No!" sighed Bootsie, "Never let it bounce." The ball rolled along the ground until it rolled into touch on the Bulldogs 5-Metre line. "Lineout!" said the referee. "Ok, Stinkey, nice and straight," said PK to

Stinkey. It didn't work, "Not straight!" said the referee. "You can have another lineout with you throwing in, or a scrum on the 15-metre line. It's your choice, captain," he said to the Rebels' captain. He chose a scrum. The scrum was set, and Bootsie couldn't believe it: the Bulldogs' scrum was good. They didn't buckle at all. The Rebels halfback picked up the ball and was pounced on by Terry the Terrier causing him to drop it forwards. "Offside, sir!" shouted the Rebels' captain. "The ball was out the halfback can tackle him," replied the referee. "Great work, Terry," Coach Van Den shouted. That was pretty much how the rest of the first half went: all in the Bulldogs favour. At halftime the score was Rebels 0, Bulldogs 10.

"Great half of rugby, boys," said Coach Van Den at the half time break. "You boys are making me so proud today. You've really listened to what I have been saying all year and it is really showing. Let's get out there, continue what you are doing and you'll win this grand final I promise you." The second half started with a huge dropkick from the Rebels' fly half. "Mine!" shouted Sticks, and he took it well. Sticks took off, his skinny little legs running fast, and Red was struggling to keep up with him. "Pass!" shouted Red, who could see what was coming. 'Smash!' Sticks ran straight into the Rebels tackler and he smashed him. Sticks lost the ball and it rolled into touch. "I-can't-brea-the," Sticks gasped, as he lay on the ground. Coach Van Den ran over to him. "Are you Ok, Sticks? That was a huge hit he put on you," the Coach said. "I-can't-brea-the," Sticks said again. "It's ok, you've just had the wind knocked out of you, that's all. Once the diaphragm muscle in your chest stops cramping, you'll be able to catch your breath again," the Coach replied with a smile. "Our Coach knows everything," Bootsie said to PK. "Diaphragm muscle? - I didn't even know I had one," Bootsie added. "Me neither," replied PK. "I wish I'd known that when I got smashed by that hooker last year. I thought I was dying," Bootsie added.

Amazingly Sticks picked himself up and slowly walked to the full back position. "That's my boy!" shouted his dad from the sideline in his thick accent. "He said that's my boy, Bootsie, in case you were wondering," said Sticks as he walked past Bootsie, trying to get his breath back. "Yeah, I know. I'm starting to understand him a bit more." replied Bootsie. The Rebels picked up their game and the score was soon level. Mad Dog had argued with the referee and had given away a penalty which the Rebels fly half had no trouble converting into points. They scored an easy try when the Bulldogs switched off just after the penalty, and the score was now Rebels 10, Bulldogs 10. The game flowed forwards and backwards but the score didn't change. The rucks were intense: bodies were flying in really hard. At one ruck, deep into the second half, the ball was stuck under a mass of players. "Pheew." The referee blew his whistle. "The ball's not coming out. Rebels were attacking. Their feed."

The scrum was set. As the ball came out and was thrown to the Rebels' fly half, Mad Dog flew off the side of the scrum and pounced on him, causing the Rebels' fly half to drop the ball. "Pheew." The referee blew his whistle. "Penalty to the Rebels. Bulldogs' flanker wasn't binding in the scrum." "What!" screamed Mad Dog. "I *was* binding. You're useless!" Mad Dog said to the referee. As soon as he had said it he knew he was in trouble.

"That's it! I've warned you already! The referee reached into his pocket. Mad Dog knew what was coming. All the Bulldogs' players knew what was coming. "That's a yellow card for you, number 6. Off you go. Ten minutes in the sin bin for backchatting," said the referee, as he showed Mad Dog the yellow card he had just pulled out of his pocket.

Mad Dog knew he had done wrong, he ran off the field and tried to run away but Coach Van Den took off after him. Mad Dog started to cry. "I'm sorry Coach. I didn't mean to say it. It just came out," Mad Dog said, expecting to be yelled at. "Hey, c'mon. No tears, hey. Rugby is a game of passion, and you've got lots of it." Coach Van Den said to Mad Dog. "But what makes you a good player is you need to be in charge of that passion. You need to keep a cool head even when every-one around you is losing theirs, ok?

"I'm not mad at you, but you let the team down when you get sent off. You need to work on this, ok Mad Dog?" "Uh–huh," was all that Mad Dog could reply as he continued to fight back the tears.

The Rebels fly half took a penalty shot at goal and kicked beautifully. Rebels 13, Bulldogs 10. "Fourteen players, and we're behind - this isn't good," Bootsie thought to himself. "If they score again, it's all over." "One minute to go!" shouted the referee. Bootsie sucked in a deep breath. "I'm going to win this game for us. I know I can do it. All year, Coach Van Den has said to believe in yourself and you can do anything," he said to himself. The ball was kicked really high by 'Super Boot' after the penalty goal. Red and Ted took off after it but weren't quick enough. The Rebels' fullback side-stepped three Bulldogs' players and was making a beeline towards Stinkey

Taylor. Bootsie started to worry. Stinkey wasn't the best tackler to have between the full back and the try line. "Don't fall for the dummy pass, Stinkey,! He's got no one on either side of him to pass to - just tackle him!," Bootsie shouted to Stinkey as he ran back to help Stinkey out. Stinkey didn't fall for the dummy pass. He stood his ground and, 'Smash!" - a great try-saving tackle. Bootsie arrived just in time to pick up the ball that the Rebels' fullback had dropped. "Advantage green!" Bootsie heard the referee say. He tucked the ball under his arm and ran as fast as he could. The first Rebels' player who tried to tackle him just bounced off him. "Tried to tackle me too high. Should have taken me around the legs," Bootsie thought to himself as he headed upfield.

Bootsie could see the Rebels hooker charging in from the side of the field. "Oh no, not you again," Bootsie said to himself. As he got closer the hooker reached out and grabbed Bootsie by his jumper, trying to pull him down. Bootsie put his arm out and pushed the Rebels' hooker with all his strength. The hooker started to fall backwards. Bootsie just kept pushing until the hooker fell to the ground, and Bootsie ran straight over the top of him. He looked up and was inside the Rebels' 22. He had Sunnie and Sione screaming for a pass just behind him, the siren sounded. "Keep running," he thought, "keep the ball in hand. If I go to ground I've got support players behind me."

As he reached the goalline he was met by three Rebels' defenders. Bootsie had momentum on his side. He barged his way through all three of them and he hit the ground, hard! Not to mention Sunnie and Sione who came piling on top of him from behind, just to make sure he got the ball down.

The referee came running over; he knelt down next to the mass of bodies on the ground. "Pheew." He blew his whistle. "Try!" Bootsie got to his feet. "Who? What?" said Bootsie. "Yes, try to that player, number 8." The referee pointed to Bootsie. He had done it. The winning try in the grand final! 'Super Boot' took the kick and it sailed over the crossbar. "Pheew." The referee blew his whistle. "That's the game!" added the referee. Final score: Rebels 13, Bulldogs 17. The South's Bulldogs under-11's had won the grand final. Bootsie had dreamed of this day. The Bulldogs' players hugged each other, Bootsie even hugged Stinkey Taylor.

What a day! What a season! Most of the clubs gave their players a small trophy for taking part in the competition, but on grand final day only players from the winning team were given a huge trophy with "Under-11's Grand Final Winners" engraved on the front of it. Bootsie had never won a grand final trophy before and was so excited to finally be holding one. He also got a blue ribbon with the word 'Captain' written on it in gold lettering for being the captain on the winning team. As Bootsie sat in the backseat on the way home from the game he looked down at his trophy with a huge smile on his face. "What a season!" Bootsie thought to himself, I can't wait for the next season to start next year. If only he knew what was in store for him the following year, he may not have been in such a hurry for it to start. But that's a whole new book.

www.bootsiebooks.com

Thanks to KooGa Rugby
www.kooga.com.au

CPSIA information can be obtained at www.ICGtesting.com
Printed in the USA
BVOW04s1814140415

396108BV00003B/55/P

9 781921 787058